© Lemniscaat b.v. Rotterdam 1994
All rights reserved
First published in the Netherlands by Lemniscaat b.v. Rotterdam
Library of Congress catalog card number: 94-70594
Published simultaneously in Canada by HarperCollins*CanadaLtd*
Printed in Belgium
First American edition, 1994

Troll's
SEARCH FOR SUMMER

Nicolas van Pallandt

FARRAR · STRAUS · GIROUX   NEW YORK

Troll was warm, but winter was so cold that when Troll stepped out to fill his water jug with snow, the wind swooped down, scooped him up, and blew him away.

It tumbled him all around
and then set him down again,
somewhere far from home.
Troll wandered for a long time,
but everywhere he looked, winter covered
the trees and the earth
and the forest slept its winter sleep.
My home is so small
and winter is so big, he thought.
In fact, the only thing
bigger than winter
is summer.
Perhaps I should look
for that instead.

So he searched and searched, but all he found was a snike with a light at the end of his tail, shivering at the foot of a rock.

'Do you know where summer is?' Troll asked him.

But Snike, being a snike, said nothing and just shivered.

So Troll tore his scarf in half and gave half to Snike.

And when Troll walked away, Snike got up and padded silently after him.

They walked and walked until they came to a hummock
where an arknark lived in a house of snow.
'Excuse me,' said Troll, 'but we're looking for summer.'
Arknark led them up a long, winding stair to a room with two
round windows and a fireplace in its center.
'That's summer.' She pointed proudly at her fire. 'Slowly it
melts my house away and when my house is completely gone,
summer escapes.'
Troll sighed and Snike said nothing and they went on their
way again.

Next they came to a dale, where a hubbin and a kweeb fished
for perch in a frozen river.
'Under the ice with the perch is the place,' said the tiny
Hubbin to Troll. 'Every year, when the cold comes,
we fish and fish until summer bites and then we pull it up,
out of the ice.'
Troll scratched his head doubtfully and Snike just stared,
with his eyes like yellow plums.
Kweeb, being a kweeb, carried on fishing.

Troll and Snike traveled on, but summer was smaller and winter was larger than Troll had ever imagined. Still Troll would not give up. Suddenly he saw an owl flying overhead. 'Maybe we could see further from up there,' Troll said to Snike. So they searched until they found a garbage can with a house behind it.

Inside the garbage can lived a mouse.
'Every year I sleep and dream of summer,' she told them.
'Until my dream comes true and I wake up.'
'But you're awake now,' said Troll, puzzled.
'I know,' she replied sadly. 'It was too cold to sleep, so I couldn't dream, and now summer will never come back.'
'Then come with us,' said Troll.
From raggedy bits they made a balloon, which they carried up to the roof of the house. They placed it over the chimney and as the hot air filled it, the balloon swelled up.

Away they flew, over
the trees and over the
fields, deep into a sky of
darkest blue.
But, though they looked,
summer was nowhere to
be seen.
They flew over the Ice
Witch, moonbathing,
and as they watched, she
shook her hair and thick
snow fell from it.
She smiled an icy wind,
which curled up and
pulled down the balloon
and spun them into a
snowdrift.

Troll and Snike and Mouse wandered through the swirling snow, growing colder and slower and wearier. But, just when they were about to give up, they saw a light shining out of the storm.

'What is it?' whispered Troll.

'What is it?' wondered Mouse.

'It's summer,' said Snike.

So they opened the door and they stepped inside.

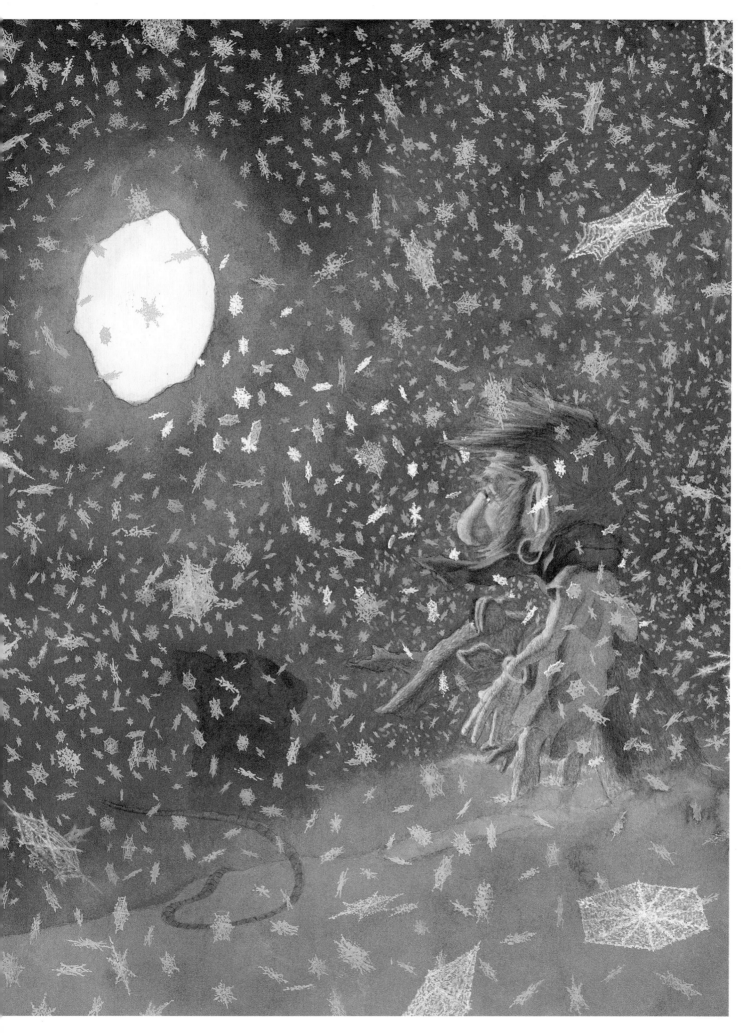

And there they slept, waiting for the day when summer would spread its fingers out from Troll's front door and cover the world.